BUSY
BEAVERS

BUSY
BEAVERS

by Lydia Dabcovich

E. P. DUTTON · NEW YORK

Published in the United States by E. P. Dutton,
2 Park Avenue, New York, N.Y. 10016,
a division of NAL Penguin Inc.
Published simultaneously in Canada by
Fitzhenry & Whiteside Limited, Toronto
Editor: Ann Durell   Designer: Riki Levinson
Printed in Hong Kong by South China Printing Co.
First Edition   W   10 9 8 7 6 5 4 3 2 1

Library of Congress Cataloging-in-Publication Data
Dabcovich, Lydia.
    Busy beavers.
    Summary: Simple text follows the activities
of a beaver family as they swim, play, and build
a sturdy dam.
    1. Beavers—Juvenile literature.   [1. Beavers]
I. Title.
QL737.R632D33   1988   599.32′32   87-27190
ISBN 0-525-44384-3

Crunch, crunch,
cut and carry,
busy beavers are at work.

Float and push,

and pile up branches,

busy beavers build a house,

safe and sound for baby beavers.

Plop, splash!

Baby beavers learn to swim.

Baby beavers play and tumble—
but—who's there?

Thump, thump!
Watch out!
Splash!

Quick, swim home.

Look . . . listen . . . sniff. . . .
Cold winds blowing,
dark clouds rolling,
a storm is coming.

Hide!

Sun's out! Hurry, hurry,
cut and carry,
fix and build.

Busy beavers are at work.